Mr. Breech

POWER &
PRECISION

by Jason Page

**PUSHING
POWER**

The mighty weightlifters are
the strongest competitors at the
Olympic Games.

ANCIENT ORIGINS

This book covers very different events at the Olympics. Some are all about strength. Others require great accuracy.

ANCIENT ORIGINS

Many of the modern Olympic events are actually thousands of years old. For example, the ancient Greeks held weightlifting competitions using huge heavy stones, while the first sporting events involving horses were chariot races. This Assyrian carving of a chariot rider is more than 2,500 years old.

Assyrian chariot

GAMES EVERYWHERE

The Olympic events in this book will be held at a wide range of venues in Sydney, from the velodrome (cycle track) to the rifle range, and the weightlifting platform to the showjumping arena. There will even be a road race through some of Sydney's suburbs!

SUPER STATS

Only 311 competitors took part in the 1896 Olympics. When the Games visit Sydney, more than 10,000 athletes will be hoping to win a medal!

GOING FOR GOLD

At the ancient Olympic Games, the winning competitors were awarded a simple crown made of olive branches. At the modern Olympics, the winners are rewarded with medals made of solid gold.

Olympic commemorative medal, 1896

EXCELLENCE IN ACTION

Competitors with disabilities have excelled at power and precision events such as archery, shooting, and horseriding. In 1952, Lis Hartel (DEN) became the first woman to win a medal in the dressage event, even though she was partially paralyzed and could not move her legs below the knee.

OLYMPICS FACT FILE

The Olympic Games were first held in Olympia, Greece, around 3,000 years ago. They took place every four years until they were abolished in A. D. 393.

A Frenchman named Pierre de Coubertin (1863–1937) revived the Games. The first modern Olympics were held in Athens in 1896.

The modern Games have been held every four years since 1896, except in 1916, 1940, and 1944, because of war. Special 10th-anniversary Games took place in 1906.

The symbol of the Olympic Games is five interlocking colored rings. They represent the five continents from which athletes come to compete.

RACE AGAINST THE CLOCK

Each competitor has to fire a certain number of arrows at the target within a set time. In the individual events, the archers are given 40 seconds to fire each arrow. In the doubles competitions, the firing time is reduced to 20 seconds per arrow.

The archer's initials must be engraved on each arrow.

This archer is using a leather "finger tab" to pull back the bowstring. Some archers wear a glove.

Archer

DID YOU KNOW?

There were no Olympic archery events between 1924 and their reintroduction in 1972. They have been part of the Olympic Games ever since.

The youngest person to win an Olympic medal in an archery event was just 14 years old. The oldest was 68!

If someone shouts "Fast!" during a competition, all the competitors must stop firing immediately.

A guard made of plastic or leather stops the bowstring from injuring the archer's arm when it is released.

Arrows are kept in a special bag called a quiver that is tied around the archer's waist.

YAMAHA

ARCHERY

People started using bows and arrows more than 20,000 years ago, which makes archery one of the oldest sports in the Olympic Games!

The archer uses an adjustable sight (called a bowsight) to aim.

Olympic archery targets

IT'S A LONG SHOT!

Archery events were included in the Olympics for the first time in 1900. Over the years, there have been many different archery events, including some that involved shooting moving targets. At the Games in Sydney, all the archers will aim for fixed targets placed 77 yards (70 meters) away.

This stabilizer balances the bow, helping the archer to hold it steady.

A woman's bow weighs more than 33 pounds (15 kg). The bow used by men weighs 48 pounds (22 kg).

TAKE A BOW

Olympic archers use a bow known as a "recurve" bow, which has ends that bend away from the archer. This type of bow was invented about 3,500 years ago.

ANIMAL OLYMPIANS

The appropriately named archerfish would be aiming for a gold medal at the Animal Olympics. It can shoot a drop of water from its mouth up to 3 feet (1 meter) away with incredible accuracy.

ARCHERY (CONTINUED)

Archers need both physical and mental strength. Lifting the heavy bow and drawing back the tight bowstring require strong muscles, while great powers of concentration are needed to focus on the target.

Archery target

An archery target has five colored circles. Each of these circles is divided into two halves by a thin line and is worth a different number of points. The closer an arrow is to the center, the more points it scores.

4 points

3 points

8 points

2 points

1 point

SPORT FOR ALL

In 1984, Neroli Fairhall (NZL) made Olympic history when she took part in the women's archery event. She was the first athlete in a wheelchair to compete at the Olympic Games. Disabled athletes also have their own Games, called the Paralympics, which will be held in Sydney two weeks after the Olympic Games.

SUPER STATS

Once fired, arrows travel through the air at around 150 mph (240 km/h). That's faster than the average speed of a Formula One racing car!

DRESSED TO IMPRESS

Justin Huish (USA) won gold medals in both the individual and team event at the 1996 Olympics. He'll be trying for another double victory when the Games visit Sydney. With his trademark mirror shades and backward

Justin Huish

baseball cap, it's not just Huish's archery skills that make him stand out from the other competitors!

Bull's-eye: 10 points

9 points

5 points

6 points

7 points

TAKING AIM

The archery target measures 4 feet (1.22 meters) across. That's about the same height as an average eight-year-old. However, from where the archers are standing, the target looks the same size as a thumbtack held at arm's length!

DID YOU KNOW?

Another word for archery is toxophily.

Disabled athletes will compete in 18 different sports at the Paralympics in Sydney. It will be the 11th time these Games have been held.

If an arrow hits the line between two scoring bands on the target, the highest score is awarded.

Allison Sydor

RIDE ON!

Allison Sydor (CAN) is the front-runner in the women's mountain bike event but she can't expect an easy ride. One of the women who will be racing against her will be Australia's very own Mary Grigson, who will have the advantage of riding on her home turf!

Miguel Martinez (FRA), known as "Mighty Mouse," is currently rated No. 1 in the world and is a stong contender for a medal.

The handlebars on a mountain bike are usually straight. There's no bell but there are two powerful brakes!

DID YOU KNOW?

♫ Mountain bikes have up to 24 gears, and some are also fitted with rear shock absorbers.

♫ The first mountain bike went on sale in 1981. Now, 70 percent of all bikes sold are mountain bikes!

♫ Cyclists in the mountain bike events are not allowed to deliberately get in each other's way and must allow faster competitors to pass them.

ON TRACK FOR VICTORY

The mountain bike events will be held at Sydney's Fairfield City Farm. Each lap of the course is 4.3 miles (6.9 km) long and takes riders on a bumpy trail through the "bush" — the Australian word for wild countryside. There, they'll have to negotiate many natural obstacles, such as ditches and fallen trees, and a steep climb!

Mountain bikes are fitted with a fork-like front suspension to help absorb bumps and knocks.

The tires on mountain bikes have deep treads to grip the slippery mud and are much wider than the tires used in other cycling events.

MOUNTAIN BIKING

All cycling competitors must wear a helmet.

Mountain bike events are like cross country running races —only on bikes! Mountain biking is the newest Olympic cycling sport, and it is making only its second appearance at the Games.

ANIMAL OLYMPIANS

When it comes to tackling tough terrain, the undisputed champion in the animal kingdom is a small goatlike antelope called the chamois. It can race up a rugged mountain, climbing up to a half mile (1,000 meters) in just 15 minutes.

A mountain bike's frame is similar in design to a road or track bike but is made of stronger materials designed to withstand the tough terrain.

Miguel Martinez

NO HELP AT ALL

Unlike other cycling sports, mountain bikers are not allowed to receive any help or assistance during the race. If their bike gets damaged, they have to repair it themselves.

CYCLING

For the road race and time trial events, Olympic cyclists will take to city streets, racing through Sydney's eastern suburbs!

RIDING IN THE SLIPSTREAM

Cyclists in the road races usually ride together in tight packs so that they can use the rider in front of them as a windbreak. This means they don't have to pedal quite so hard to keep up! The technique, known as "drafting," is forbidden in the time trial races.

SUPER STATS

The longest road race ever was held at the 1912 Games in Stockholm. It was 198 miles (320 km) long. That's like cycling from London to Paris!

Men's individual road race

TIME TRIAL

In the time trials, competitors start the race one at a time, with a gap of 90 seconds between each rider. The winner is the cyclist who completes the course in the fastest time, not the one who reaches the finish first. The men's event is 29 miles (46.8 km) long and the women's is 19 miles (31.2 km).

ON YER BIKE!

The bikes used in road races are much lighter than mountain bikes and have much narrower tires. The handlebars are curved, enabling riders to lean forward in the saddle, reducing wind resistance and increasing their speed. Road race bikes have eight gears.

DID YOU KNOW?

Cyclists on the same national team are allowed to share food and swap tools during the road race!

In both the road race and the time trials, helpers in support vehicles may follow the riders and make emergency repairs to their bikes.

At the 1896 Olympics, the road race was won by a Greek rider who borrowed a bike from a spectator after crashing his own!

The reigning women's time trials champion is Zulifiya Zabirova (RUS).

ROAD RACE

The road races are straightforward—but very long! All the competitors start at the same time, and the winner is the first to cross the finish line. Each lap of the course is 11 miles (18 km). Men complete 13 laps, and women complete 7 laps.

Zulifiya Zabirova

Women's road race: Jeannie Longo-Ciprelli (FRA) **Women's time trial:** Zulifiya Zabirova (RUS)

Velodrome, 1996 Olympics

DROME SWEET HOME

All the track events are held inside a specially built cycling track called a velodrome. The surface of the velodrome is made of wood and slopes so that the outside of the track is much higher than the inside. One lap of the velodrome is 274 yards (250 meters).

DID YOU KNOW?

Cycling is one of only five sports that have been included in every modern Olympic Games. The others are fencing, gymnastics, athletics, and swimming.

Cycling and canoeing are the only Olympic events that are timed to 1,000th of a second!

The velodrome used in the 1964 Olympics in Tokyo cost around $800,000 to build. It was only used for four days and then knocked down!

Chris Boardman (GBR) won the men's individual pursuit in 1992 on this bike. It weighed just 18 pounds (8 kg).

Boardman's bike seat was higher than the handlebars.

To help reduce drag, the back wheel on most track bikes is solid (it's known as a disc wheel). The front wheel usually has just three spokes.

REIGNING OLYMPIC CHAMPIONS: **Men's point race**: Silvio Martinello (ITA) **Men's individual pursuit**: Andrea Collinelli (ITA) **Team pursuit**: France **Madison**: This event will be held for the first time at the 2000 Games.

CYCLING (CONTINUED)

There are 12 track events for cyclists —
four for women and eight for men.

Track riders wear aerodynamic helmets designed to reduce wind resistance, or "drag," and help them travel faster.

NAME THAT RACE

Individual pursuit: Two riders start on opposite sides of the track with the aim of catching their opponent. If, after 16 laps for men and 12 laps for women, neither rider has been caught, the cyclist who crosses his or her own finish line first is the winner.

Team pursuit: Similar to the individual pursuit except that this race is contested by two teams of four riders. Only men compete in this event.

Points race: Male competitors race for 160 laps and women for 100 laps. At the end of every 10th lap, they are awarded points according to their position: five for first, three for second, two for third, and one for fourth. The winner is the rider with the most points.

Madison: A team version of the points race, for men only, which takes place over 240 laps. The two-man teams are usually made up of a sprinter and a long-distance cyclist, who take turns racing against the opposing team.

Chris Boardman

SUPER STATS

France has won 73 medals in the Olympic cycling events, including 32 golds. That's more than any other nation! In second place, with 54 medals, is Italy. Great Britain is third with 46.

Women's points race: Nathalie Lancien (FRA)
Women's individual pursuit: Antonélla Bellutti (ITA)

CYCLING
(CONTINUED)

The remaining track events are time trials and sprints. Time trials focus on speed, while sprints test riders' cunning as well as their strength.

BATTLE OF WITS

Sprinters, such as Olympic champion Jens Fielder (GER), use cunning tactics to win. The riders usually begin very slowly and may even stop on the second lap in an attempt to get into the best position for the sudden race to the finish.

ANIMAL OLYMPIANS

Jens Fielder achieved a record speed of more than 43 mph (70 km/h) during the 1992 Olympics, but that's nothing compared to the top speed of a sprinting cheetah. These super-speedy big cats can race along at around 62 mph (100 km/h).

Jens Fielder

REIGNING OLYMPIC CHAMPIONS: Men's 1-km time trial: Florian Rousseau (FRA)   **Men's sprint:** Jens Fielder (GER)
Olympic sprint: This event will be held for the first time at the 2000 Games.   **Keirin:** This event will be held for the first time at the 2000 Games.

NAME THAT RACE

Time trial: Cyclists race against the clock, and the rider with the fastest time wins. The men's race is four laps, and the women's race is two laps.

Sprint: A three-lap race between two riders. However, the riders spend the first two laps jockeying for position before making a final dash over the last 200 meters to the finish line.

Olympic sprint: Two three–man teams race against each other for three laps, and the fastest team wins. Only men compete in this event.

Keirin (kay rin): For men only, this is an eight-lap race but competitors remain behind a motorcycle for the first 5.5 laps. The motorcycle gradually speeds up from 16 mph (25 km/h) to 25 mph (40 km/h) before leaving the track and allowing the cyclists to sprint to the finish.

NO BRAKES!

The bikes used in track events don't have any brakes! They also have just one gear. This means that cyclists must pedal all the time to keep moving.

Reigning men's time trials champ, Florian Rousseau (FRA), holds the gold medal he won at the 1996 Olympics.

DID YOU KNOW?

The 1896 Olympics included a 12-hour track race. Only two contestants managed to finish the event, and it was never held again!

Until 1972, there was a cycling event for tandems—bicycles ridden by two people.

During the semifinal of the men's sprint in 1964, both riders stood still for more than 21 minutes, waiting for the other to make his move!

Women's sprint: Felicia Ballanger (FRA)
Women's 500 meters time trial: This event will be held for the first time at the 2000 Games.

DID YOU KNOW?

In 1956, when the Olympics were last held in Australia, all the equestrian events took place in Sweden. This was because Australia's strict quarantine laws wouldn't allow competitors' horses into the country!

In 1932, the course was so difficult that no team managed to complete it, and no medals were awarded!

In the event of a tie, the course is rearranged and the competitors are timed as they go around again. This is called a "jump off." If they end up with the same score again, the rider with the best time wins.

EQUAL OPPORTUNITIES

Equestrian sports do not have separate events for men and women. All the competitions are open to riders (and horses!) of both sexes. As well as the individual event, there is also a team event in which four riders from the same country compete together.

Upright

The showjumping arena is 131 yards (120m) long and 88 yards (80m) wide — longer and wider than a soccer field.

Showjumping arena

A FAULTLESS PERFORMANCE

In 1992, Ludger Beerbaum (GER) became only the fourth competitor in the history of the Games to win the gold after picking up no penalty points at all.

Ludger Beerbaum

REIGNING OLYMPIC CHAMPIONS: Individual jumping: Ulrich Kirchhoff (on Jus de Pommes) (GER)

SHOWJUMPING

*T*here are three different horse riding competitions, called equestrian events, at the Olympics. So saddle up and get ready to gallop into number one—showjumping!

Water jump

Spread

Combination

IT'S ALL YOUR FAULT

In showjumping, horse and rider have to go around a course that contains at least 15 jumps. The idea is to clear all the jumps in the right order within the required time limit, picking up as few penalty points as possible. These penalties are called "faults," and they are awarded for a range of different mistakes, for example, when the horse knocks down fences or refuses to jump.

LEARN THE LINGO

Courses are constructed using four basic types of jump.

Combinations: These are made up of two or three jumps placed a few strides apart.

Spreads: These are wider than uprights but also lower.

Uprights: These are the tallest jumps and may be up to 5.6 feet (1.7 meters) high.

Water jumps: These are shallow water-filled troughs that may be up to 14.8 feet (4.5 meters) wide.

Team jumping: Germany

DRESSAGE

The word "dressage" comes from a French word meaning "training." This event is all about testing the riders' control of their horses.

DOING THE ROUNDS

The individual competition consists of three rounds. In the first two, competitors must perform a set routine of moves and maneuvers. The third is a freestyle round, which gives the riders a chance to show off their skills by performing their own routines set to music.

ANIMAL OLYMPIANS

The most successful horse in the history of the Games was named Rembrandt. Between 1988 and 1992, it won no fewer than four gold medals in the dressage events!

SOLDIER ON

Until 1952, only commissioned officers in the armed forces were allowed to compete in the Olympic dressage events. This rule was strictly enforced. When it was discovered that one member of the winning Swedish team in 1948 had a lower rank, the team was disqualified.

REIGNING OLYMPIC CHAMPIONS: **Individual dressage:** Isabell Werth (on Gigolo) (GER)

Saluting the judges, Atlanta 1996

MAKING YOUR POINT

Each dressage competition is scored by five judges, who sit in different positions around the arena. They award the horse and rider points out of 10 for each move. Basic dressage moves include the pirouette (a tight turn in which the horse keeps one of its back legs in the same spot), the passage (a very slow, elegant trot), and the piaffe (trotting in place).

Isabell Werth

LOOK SMART

As you can see from this picture of the reigning champion, Isabell Werth (GER), competitors in dressage events must follow a strict dress code. This includes top hat and tails, a white shirt, polished black boots, and white pants. Riders who work in the police or armed forces are allowed to wear their uniforms.

DID YOU KNOW?

Lorna Johnstone (GBR) became the oldest woman to compete in the Olympics when she took part in the dressage in 1972, five days after her 70th birthday!

Riders are forbidden to communicate with their horse by making noises.

Contestants can lose points if their horse swishes its tail or puts its ears back!

DID YOU KNOW?

❓ In 1936, one competitor fell off his horse during the cross country run and took almost 3 hours to catch it. He ended up with more than 18,000 penalty points!

❓ In the event of a draw at the end of the three-day event, the team or rider with the best cross country score is the winner.

❓ Riders must use the same horse in all three parts of the three-day event.

BIG BREAKS

Three-day eventing is by far the toughest of the equestrian events — as the medical reports prove! At least four Olympic gold medalists have stood on the winners' podium with broken bones. They include Wendy Schaeffer, a member of the victorious Australian team at the 1996 Olympics. When asked about her injury, Schaeffer replied: "It's nothing drastic, just a broken leg!"

BUSY DAYS

The individual competition is spread over three days. The team event takes four days. There are four riders in each team. On day one (and day two in the team event), competitors take part in the dressage competition. This is followed by a speed and endurance day and showjumping on the final day.

Sally Clark (NZL) won a silver medal in the individual three-day event at the 1996 Games.

THREE-DAY EVENT

The three-day event combines dressage and showjumping with a grueling cross country run. It's the ultimate challenge for horse and rider and tests their skill and stamina to the limits.

CROSS COUNTRY

The cross country ride forms the final part of what is called the speed and endurance day. The aim is to avoid penalty points by jumping the obstacles and finishing within the required time. The day is made up of four parts:

A. Flat roads and tracks: 2.7 miles (4.4 km)

B. Steeplechase (horses must jump nine fences): 1.93 miles (3.11 km)

C. Flat roads and tracks: 4.91 miles (7.92 km)

D. Rough country with up to 35 obstacles, including water jumps and ditches: 4.59 miles (7.41 km).

Mark Todd (NZL) won four Olympic medals in the three-day event between 1984 and 1992.

Mark Todd

SUPER STATS

German competitors have dominated the equestrian events, winning no fewer than 31 gold medals. At the 1936 Olympics, they produced the one-and-only "clean sweep" — winning gold in all six events. Switzerland has won 17 golds, and France has won 11.

Sally Clark

Team: Australia

SHOOTING: PISTOL

Are you ready? Then get very steady to take a look at the pistol shooting competitions. In these events, the slightest wobble can cost you a gold medal!

QUICK-FIRE ROUNDS

In the men's rapid fire event, competitors have only a short time to take aim and shoot. In the first round, they are allowed 8 seconds to fire five shots at five different targets. The time limit is reduced to 6 seconds in the second round, and 4 seconds in the final round.

Olga Klochneva (RUS) is the reigning Olympic champion in the women's air pistol event.

Air pistols use compressed air to fire a small pellet, instead of a bullet, at the target.

A computer-generated image of the target allows competitors to see where each shot hits and then figure their score.

ANIMAL OLYMPIANS

The sharp shooting star of the animal kingdom is the spitting cobra. When threatened, the snake shoots poisonous venom out of its mouth with deadly accuracy. It always aims for its enemy's eyes and can score a direct hit at a range of more than 7 feet (2 meters)!

ONE CHOICE LEFT

Károly Takács was a member of Hungary's world-champion pistol-shooting team in 1938 when his right hand was blown off by a grenade during an army training exercise. Takács was determined that the accident wouldn't end his shooting career. He spent 10 years teaching himself to shoot left-handed and went on to win two Olympic gold medals!

Ear protectors block out any distracting sounds and help competitors to concentrate.

Competitors wear blinders around their eyes to help them focus on the target.

Olga Klochneva

DID YOU KNOW?

Pierre de Coubertin, the founder of the modern Olympic Games, was a former French pistol-shooting champion.

Women competed in the shooting events for the first time in 1968. Women-only events were introduced in 1984.

Pistol shooters must hold the gun with one hand only.

ON TARGET

The distance of the target depends on the event. In air pistol competitions, it's 33 feet (10m) away. In the rapid fire and sports pistol events, it's 82 feet (25m) away. In the free pistol, it's 164 feet (50m) away. Each target consists of 10 rings. Each ring is worth a different score, from 1-10 points.

Rapid fire targets

Men's rifle competition (prone)

TAKING UP POSITION

In the air rifle and running target events, competitors stand up to shoot. In the "prone" event, they shoot lying down on the ground. In the "three-position" event, they fire from standing, kneeling, and lying positions. Whatever the position, the competitors are forbidden to let their rifles touch or rest against any other object.

DID YOU KNOW?

🏋 In 1920, 72-year-old Oscar Swahn (SWE) became the oldest Olympic medalist in any sport when he won silver in one of the rifle events.

🏋 To a sharpshooter, the bull's-eye on the shooting target looks as big as a stop sign.

🏋 The most successful marksman in the history of the Games was Carl Osburn (USA), who won 11 medals (five gold, four silver, and two bronze) between 1912 and 1924.

Shooters do not wear clothing with straps, laces, or seams.

BULL'S-EYE

At the Games in 1956, Gerald Ouellette (CAN) scored 600 points in the prone event — the highest possible score! However, his score was never officially recognized because the rifle range turned out to be 4.9 feet (1.5 meters) too short. The first official perfect score of 600 was eventually achieved in the prone event by Miroslav Varaga (TCH) in 1988.

REIGNING OLYMPIC CHAMPIONS: **MEN: Running target:** Yang Ling (CHN) **Air rifle:** Artem Khadzhibekov (RUS) **Small-bore rifle (prone):** Christian Klees (GER)

SHOOTING: RIFLE

Six different events involve shooting with rifles. Two of the events are for women and four are for men.

This black square blocks the vision from the eye the competitor isn't using.

Yuri Fedkine

Yuri Fedkine (EUN) won the men's air rifle event at the 1992 Games.

Shooters usually wear a glove on the hand that holds the rifle but not on the hand that pulls the trigger.

MOVING TARGET

In the running target event, competitors have to shoot a moving target as it slides across a gap between two protective walls. The target moves at two speeds — on a slow run, the competitors have 5 seconds to shoot; on a fast run, they have just 2.5 seconds! This is the only event in which competitors are allowed to aim using a telescopic sight.

SUPER STATS

The United States has shot to the top of the winners' table in the shooting events, with 43 gold medals. In second place is Russia/Soviet Union with 25 golds. Norway is third with 16 wins.

Small-bore rifle (three position): Jean-Pierre Amat (FRA)   **WOMEN:** Air rifle: Renata Mauer (POL)   Small-bore rifle (three position): Alexandra Ivosev (YUG)

SHOOTING: SHOT GUN

At the 1900 Olympics, people shot at real pigeons. Fortunately, the only pigeons people will be shooting at the Games in Sydney will be clay ones!

WATCH THE BIRDIE!

Competitors in the Olympic shot gun events shoot at saucer-shaped targets known as "clay pigeons," or "clays" for short. Clays are catapulted through the air at great speed by a device called a trap. The aim is to shoot the clays before they go out of range or hit the ground.

GUNS WITHOUT BULLETS

The guns used in other Olympic shooting events fire a single bullet or pellet, but a shot gun fires lots of little round balls called "shot." As these balls fly through the air, they start to spread out, covering a much wider area than just one bullet. This is why shot guns are used to hit difficult, fast-moving targets at close range.

READY, AIM, FIRE!

At Sydney, both men and women will compete in three different types of shot gun events:

1. Trap: The clays are released one at a time, and contestants get two shots at each one.

2. Double trap: Two clays are released at the same time, and contestants get only one shot at each one.

3. Skeet: Contestants move around, shooting from eight different positions or "stations" on the course. The clays are released two at a time, and competitors are allowed one shot at each.

Women's double trap event

DID YOU KNOW?

♒ Clay pigeons aren't made of clay at all, but from a mixture of limestone and tar.

♒ Clays fly out of the traps at 53 mph (85 km/h) — as fast as a real pigeon can fly at top speed!

♒ In trap and double trap events, the clay is released as soon as the competitor shouts "pull!" In skeet events, there can be a delay of up to 3 seconds.

Ennio Falco

Ennio Falco (ITA) celebrates his victory in the skeet competition at the 1996 Games. To be a champion in the shot gun events requires lightning reactions as well as super accuracy.

LEARN THE LINGO

Birds: another word for clays

Cartridge: shot gun ammunition

Choke: This part of the gun determines how wide the shot spreads.

Pull!: competitors shout out "pull!" when they are ready to shoot

Trap : a machine that launches the clays into the air

DID YOU KNOW?

♫ New weight categories will be introduced at the Games in Sydney. This means each winner will set an Olympic record!

♫ Ancient Egyptian wall paintings from 4,000 years ago show weightlifters using bags filled with sand.

♫ At the 1896 Olympic Games, there was a weightlifting event that only allowed the use of one arm!

THE SNATCH

Naim Suleymanoglu

In the snatch, competitors must lift the weight above their head in one single movement. As they hoist the weight above them, they squat down underneath it and lock their arms. Then, keeping the weight at arm's length above their head, they stand up straight. Here, three-time Olympic champion Naim Suleymanoglu (TUR) shows how it's done.

THE CLEAN & JERK

In the clean and jerk event, competitors lift the weight above their head in two stages. First, they raise the bar to their chests. This must be done in a single, "clean" movement. Then they thrust the bar over their heads with a quick "jerk" movement and stand up straight.

MEN'S WEIGHTLIFTING

*T**he mighty weightlifters are the strongest competitors at the Olympic Games.***

WEIGHT FOR IT!

Weightlifters at the Olympics compete in different weight classes according to how heavy they are. However, the rules in each event are the same. All competitors must perform two different sorts of lift — called the "snatch" and the "clean and jerk." The heaviest weight they manage to lift in the first category is added to the heaviest one in the second category to give their final score. And whoever has the highest total is the winner!

SUPER STATS

The strongest weightlifters can lift three times their own body weight using the clean and jerk technique!

HOLD EVERYTHING!

Competitors are allowed three attempts at each lift. They are watched by three judges, who decide whether the attempt is successful. A valid lift is when the weight is held above the head with the arms out straight. The feet must be in a straight line, and contestants must be standing still. Sometimes the weight is just too heavy. The legs buckle, and down goes the weight *and* the competitor, as happened here to Manfred Norlinger (GER)!

Manfred Norlinger

76 kg: Pablo Lara (CUB) **83 kg:** Pyrros Dimas (GRE) **91 kg:** Aleksey Petrov (RUS) **99 kg:** Akakide Kakhiashgilis (GRE) **108 kg:** Timur Taimazov (UKR) **108 kg-plus:** Andrei Chemerkin (RUS)

WOMEN'S WEIGHTLIFTING

When the Games visit Sydney, women will compete in the weightlifting events for the first time in Olympic history.

Peng Li Ping (CHN)

ANIMAL OLYMPIANS

When it comes to weightlifting, ants are in a league of their own. Despite their small size, these tiny insects can lift and carry things 50 times their own body weight. If humans could do the same, heavyweight weightlifters would be able to pick up more than 5 tons with ease. That's as heavy as five family cars!

POWDER UP

The part of the bar that the competitors hold has a rough, bevelled surface to keep it from slipping in their hands. Weightlifters are also allowed to put chalk dust on their hands to improve their grip.

COLOR CODE

The different weights used in weightlifting are color-coded. But when figuring out how much a competitor is lifting, don't forget to add on 33 pounds (15 kg) for the bar and 11 pounds (5 kg) for the two collars that hold the weights in place.

RED	55 lb / 25 kg	**BLUE**	44 lb / 20 kg
YELLOW	33 lb / 15 kg	**GREEN**	22 lb / 10 kg
WHITE	11 lb / 5 kg	**BLACK**	5.5 lb / 2.5 kg

The women's weightlifting event will be contested for the first time at the Olympics in 2000.

Xia Yang (CHN)

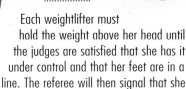

THAT'S THE WAY TO DO IT!

Each weightlifter must hold the weight above her head until the judges are satisfied that she has it under control and that her feet are in a line. The referee will then signal that she may put the weight down. Competitors must lower the bar to waist level before releasing their grip and letting go.

GREAT EXPECTATIONS

China is expected to do extremely well in the women's weightlifting events at the Sydney Games. Some people are even predicting that the Chinese may win gold medals in all seven women's events. Other nations to watch are Bulgaria and Taiwan.

DID YOU KNOW?

At the Games in 1924, one weightlifting competitor was only 13 years old!

Weightlifter Harold Sakata (USA), a silver medalist at the 1948 Olympics, went on to star as Oddjob in the James Bond film Goldfinger.

After each successful lift, the weight on the bar must be increased by at least 5.5 pounds (2.5 kg), unless the competitor is attempting to break the world record.

This means that the first Olympic records in this sport will be set in Sydney.

INDEX

Acknowledgements
We would like to thank Ian Hodge, Rosalind Beckman, Jackie Gaff, and Elizabeth Wiggans for their assistance. Cartoons by John Alston.
Copyright © 2000 *ticktock* Publishing Ltd.
First published in Great Britain by ticktock Publishing Ltd., The Offices in the Square, Hadlow, Tonbridge, Kent TN11 0DD, Great Britain.
Printed in Hong Kong.
Picture Credits: t = top, b = bottom, l = left, r = right, OFC = outside front cover, OBC = outside back cover, IFC = inside front cover
Allsport; IFC, OFC, 3tr, 4/5 (main pic), 5tr, 6/7c, 7tr, 8tl, 8/9c, 11bl, 10/11 (main pic), 12tl, 12/13 (main pic), 14/15 (main pic), 15b, 16/17 (main pic), 16br, 18/19 (main pic), 19tr, 21r, 20/21 (main pic), 22/23c, 23br, 24tl, 24/25 (main pic), 26/27 (main pic), 26t, 28/29b, 28/29t, 30/31 (main pic), 30/31c. Image select; 2/3c. Picture research by Image Select.
Library of Congress Cataloging-in-Publication Data
Page, Jason.
Power and precision : cycling, equestrian, shooting, and lots, lots more / by Jason Page.
p. cm. — (Zeke's Olympic pocket guide)
Summary: Describes the riding and shooting events of the Olympic Games and previews the athletic competition at the 2000 Summer Olympics in Sydney, Australia.
Includes index.
ISBN 0-8225-5050-4 (pbk. : alk. paper)
1. Sports--Juvenile literature. 2. Olympics--Juvenile literature. [1. Sports. 2. Olympics.] I. Title. II. Series.
GV721.53 . P35 2000
796.48--dc21
00--008097